THE SOUR GRAPE

To my grandmother, Barbara
—J.J.

For Amy and Annemarie
—P.O.

ISBN 978-1-5461-2358-3

12 11 10 9 8 7 6 5 4 3 2 1   24 25 26 27 28 29

Printed in the U.S.A.   40

First Scholastic printing, January 2024

The artist used scanned watercolor textures and digital paint to create the illustrations for this book.

THE SOUR GRAPE

From the #1 *New York Times* Bestselling Team
JORY JOHN AND PETE OSWALD

SCHOLASTIC INC.

I'm a grape.
A sour grape.

Grrrrrrr!

If somebody upsets me, I'll remember it.
If somebody wrongs me, I won't forget it.
If somebody insults me, I'll never ignore it. Nope.

See that banana over there? That banana slipped and bumped into me. So I'm holding a grudge!

See that orange? That orange didn't call me back for a week. Grudge!

See that lime? That lime borrowed my scarf and never returned it. Grudge!

I suppose I've got pretty thin skin for a grape.
Nobody steps on this grape!

Grrrrrrrrrrrrrrrr!

Granted, it wasn't always this way . . .

We all lived on a vine. Sure, it was a bit claustrophobic. Especially when we were trying to get ready in the morning.

But my family was ripe with humor, goodwill, and warmth. We did our best with what we had.

My grandparents visited on the weekends. We'd stroll in the sun and they'd teach us what they knew.
They said that it takes a bunch to raise a seed.
They said that good grapes roll their own way in life.
They told us to be kind, forgiving, considerate, and grateful.
"Or *grapeful*," my grandpa said with a wink.

"Above all, no matter what life throws at you—and there will be a lot—try to stay sweet," my grandma said.
"Indeed," we said in response.

And for a while, I *was* the sweetest of the sweet.
I said, "Please." I said, "Thank you." I brushed aside life's
little annoyances. I knew how good I had it.

But then one day, something changed in me.

It was my birthday.
I had rigorously and vigorously planned a big party for weeks.
I'd sent out invitations with the date prominently displayed.

Get this: I had a Ferris wheel, a magician, and hayrides.
I had snacks upon snacks upon snacks.
The highlight of the party, though, was a fireworks display,
which would happen at sundown.

I stood out front and waited for folks to arrive.
I had a gigantic smile on my face.

I waited.

Everybody was a little late, it seemed. No big deal.
No big whoop.

So I waited.

A tumbleweed rolled by.

A coyote howled in the distance.

"Sigh."

Awoooooooooo!

The sun sank behind
the hills.

And I waited.

Nobody showed up. And I mean *nobody*.

By the time the fireworks show started—with me as the sole spectator—I was scowling.

After that, my personality became something else entirely.

I went from a sweet grape . . .

to a bitter grape . . .

to a snappy grape.

Who moved my chair?!

Finally, I became a sour grape.

Grrrrrrrr!

I started holding minor grudges that, eventually, became *major* grudges.

I scowled so much that my face got all squishy.

I took my grumpiness out on others.

And that's just how it's been.
Day after day.
Week after week.
Month after month.
Grudge after grudge.

But something happened recently that changed my thinking . . .

I was getting ready to meet up with my friend Lenny, the only fellow I know who's as sour as I am.

Lenny and I usually go to the park, where we sit on a bench and rant about stuff.

But just as I was heading out the door, I bumped my knee.

"Oof!"

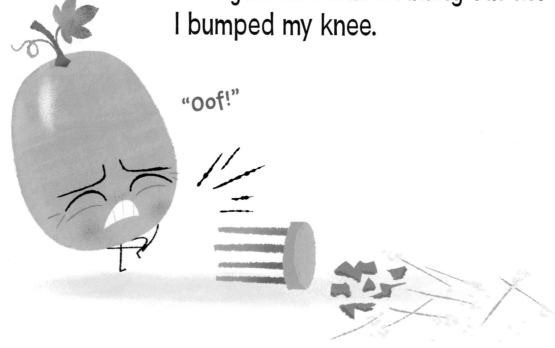

After I bandaged myself up,
I discovered I had a flat tire.

Then I missed the bus
and the *next* bus was late.

Finally, I got off at the wrong stop.

By the time I arrived at the park, it was getting dark.
Lenny was fuming and furious, with a frown and
a furrowed forehead.
His face looked all squishy.

We agreed to meet at exactly four o'clock.
You're three hours late!

I tried to explain why I was so tardy, but Lenny wouldn't listen. He'd already made up his mind. He'd formed a huge grudge and he wouldn't budge!

I couldn't believe it!

How unfair, I thought!
How ridiculous, I thought!
How . . . um . . . how similar to the way *I* would react.

"Hmmmmmmmmm."

Lenny was pretty worked up. He was pacing back and
forth, emitting occasional grumbles. His tone was tart.

So I gave him a
little space.

Besides, it was nice out. I noticed the sky changing colors,
the melodic chirping of the birds, the evening breeze, the
buzz of the park's insects coming alive at night.
I suddenly felt grateful. And peaceful. And calm.

Had I been missing all this simple beauty because I was too busy complaining?

Meanwhile, ol' Lenny stormed off, muttering something about "disrespect" and "lack of consideration." I'm pretty sure I heard him add a "Grrr!" too.

I walked home. I pulled a dusty box out from under my bed. There were old family photos inside.

I spotted myself in one of the pictures. I was so sweet!

I knew that little grape from the photo was still a big part of me, deep down.

It would just take some work to get back there again.

And that was the exact moment I found the invitation I had sent out for my infamous birthday party. The one where nobody showed up. It said May 31. But wait . . . wait a minute here . . . my birthday was on May **21**. Alas, I'd told everyone to come on the *wrong day*!

Gulp!
It was all my fault.
I realized nobody's perfect. Not even *me*.

After that day, I started noticing other things, too.
Like . . . how remaining sour all the time is so *draining*.
I'd wasted so much energy holding grudges when I
could've easily cleared the air if I'd felt hurt.

And yes, I still get upset from time to time. But that's okay!

Because now I talk, and I listen, and I work things out instead of just walking away.

My sourness is fading.
I'm letting go of all my grudges.
And hey, it's working.

Orange you glad we got to catch up?

I'm so *grapeful* that we did!

Sure, sometimes I still let out a little
"Grrrrrr" when I'm frustrated.

Like this:

Grrrrrrr!

But then I move on.
My face is less squishy, too.

You know what?

If you look at things in the right sort of way—and if you remember to be kind, considerate, forgiving, and grateful—life really *can* be pretty sweet.

Yes, indeed.

JORY JOHN and
PETE OSWALD

are the #1 *New York Times* bestselling creators of *The Bad Seed*, *The Good Egg*, *The Cool Bean*, *The Couch Potato*, *The Smart Cookie*, and other books in their internationally acclaimed series. Jory and Pete also collaborated on the *New York Times* bestselling *The Good Egg Presents: The Great Eggscape!*, *The Bad Seed Presents: The Good, the Bad, and the Spooky*, and *The Cool Bean Presents: As Cool as It Gets*. Jory writes at home in Oregon and Pete illustrates in his California studio.